ABT

FRIE
OF ACPL
P9-CCZ-282

THE Christmas Scrapbook

Also by Philip Gulley

Fiction

Home to Harmony

Just Shy of Harmony

Christmas in Harmony

Signs and Wonders

Life Goes On

A Change of Heart

Nonfiction

Front Porch Tales

Hometown Tales

For Everything a Season

If Grace Is True (with James Mulholland)

If God Is Love (with James Mulholland)

Philip Gulley

In addition to writing, Philip Gulley also enjoys the ministry of speaking.
If you would like more information, please contact:

David Leonards
3612 North Washington Boulevard, Indianapolis, IN 46205–3592
317–926–7566 / ieb@prodigy.net

If you would like to correspond directly with Philip Gulley, please send mail to:

Philip Gulley
c/o HarperSanFrancisco
353 Sacramento St., Suite 500
San Francisco, CA 94111

HarperCollins books may be purchased for educational, business, or sales promotional use. For information please write: Special Markets Department, HarperCollins Publishers, 10 East 53rd Street, New York, NY 10022.

HarperCollins Web site: http://www.harpercollins.com
HarperCollins®, ®, and HarperSanFrancisco™ are
trademarks of HarperCollins Publishers.

FIRST EDITION

Library of Congress Cataloging-in-Publication Data
Gulley, Phillip.
The Christmas scrapbook : a Christmas in Harmony novella /
Philip Gulley. — 1st ed.
p. cm.
ISBN-13: 978–0–06–073661–5
ISBN-10: 0–06–073661–5
1. Harmony (Ind.: Imaginary place)—Fiction. 2. Married women—Fiction.
3. Scrapbooks—Fiction. 4. Indiana—Fiction. 5. Quakers—Fiction. I. Title.
PS3557.U449S36 2005
813'.54—dc22 2005040360

05 06 07 08 09 HAD 10 9 8 7 6 5 4 3 2 1

CONTENTS

ONE
Suspicious Minds

Barbara Gardner had been suspicious of her husband, Sam, for some time. Her doubts had begun in September, when he'd been absent from their home on Wednesday evenings, purportedly to attend a men's group over in Cartersburg.

"What kind of men's group?" she'd asked him when he'd told her his plans.

"Oh, you know, a men's group. Hey, it's not all that easy being a man these days," Sam said, a note of defensiveness creeping into his voice.

Sam Gardner has never been a good liar, a serious detriment for a minister, who must often fudge things a bit in order to keep people happy.

"So what does one do in a men's group?" Barbara asked.

"Uh, well, we talk."

"About what?"

"Oh, you know, plumbing and garages and power tools mostly."

In fact, Sam Gardner was enrolled in a scrapbooking class, making a picture scrapbook for Barbara for Christmas.

In early August, he'd read an advertisement in the *Harmony Herald* about a scrapbooking class at the community college in Cartersburg and the next day, determined to redeem a dreadful history of gift giving, had enrolled in the class.

Unschooled in the methods of trickery and deceit, he hadn't crafted a reasonable excuse until it was too late. When, on the first night of class, Barbara had asked him to explain his absence, the first thought that came to mind was the men's group. He wished now he'd told her it was a Bible study, then suggested she attend also, which would have nipped her curiosity in the bud.

It hadn't taken Sam long to realize he'd made a serious mistake. He was the only man in a class of twenty. His teacher, a Mrs. Hilda Gruber, had been a drill sergeant in her previous life (Sam reckoned for the Nazis), and the other students avoided him like the plague, lest by taint of association they incur Mrs. Gruber's wrath.

In early October, she'd asked Sam to stay after class.

"It pains me to tell you this," she said in a grim voice, pronouncing each word with Teutonic precision, "but you are in grave danger of failing this class."

"Failing? How can I fail? I thought this class was just for fun."

"It that so? Well, perhaps that explains your problem. Scrapbooking is a serious artistic endeavor, not to be undertaken lightly." She opened Sam's scrapbook. "Just look at this. Your glue work is atrocious, and your scissor performance is simply deplorable."

"I never was very good with glue," Sam admitted. "When I was in the fourth grade, I accidentally glued my hand to my head. They had to take to me the hospital to get me unstuck." He pointed to a faint white scar on his forehead. "See that?"

Mrs. Gruber clucked her tongue in disgust. "If I don't see an improvement in the next several weeks, I'll have to give you an F."

"Perhaps I could do some extra credit?" Sam suggested.

"Mr. Gardner, your scrapbooking deficiencies are such that no amount of extra credit could improve your standing. Your only hope is to discard," she paused, searching for the right word to properly convey her revulsion, "this abomination and start anew."

"Throw it away? You want me to throw it away?"

"It would be the Christian thing to do, so as not to inflict it on anyone else."

Sam hung his head. "I was making it for my wife for Christmas," he said dejectedly.

Mrs. Gruber sighed.

"Last year I got her a ceramic pelican," Sam volunteered.

"Whatever for?"

"To set on the windowsill over the kitchen sink. It holds a dishwashing sponge in its bill."

"That poor, poor woman." She closed the offending scrapbook, then pointed her finger squarely at Sam. "Mr. Gardner, I want you to arrive an hour early next week and plan to stay an hour after. I'll see if I can't salvage this scrapbook. But do not get your hopes up. One person can do only so much, after all."

Sam drove home, despondent over this turn of events. He'd

been deeply pleased with himself for securing a gift for his wife so far in advance. His usual custom had been to stew for the months preceding Christmas, then, still clueless, descend on Kivett's Five and Dime on December 24, where he would paw over the dregs no one else had wanted. But this year had been different. He'd stayed up late, after Barbara had gone to bed, rummaging through the shoe boxes where they kept their photographs, picking the cream of the crop for the scrapbook. He'd had duplicate copies made at a one-hour photo shop in Cartersburg so she wouldn't be the wiser.

Weeks of scheming, lying, gluing, and cutting down the drain.

Barbara was seated at the kitchen table working a crossword puzzle when he walked in the kitchen door. "Hi, honey," she said. "How was your men's group?"

"Fine, just fine."

"So what did you talk about tonight?"

"Uh, riding mowers."

"You spent two hours talking about lawn mowers?"

"Well, not just that. We had to take attendance too. And pay our dues. And . . ." He paused to consider what else might conceivably happen at a men's meeting. "And we talked about football some too."

Barbara frowned.

"That sounds odd. I was talking with Deena Morrison about it and she said men's groups talk about their feelings and have book discussions."

"My group doesn't do much of that."

"She also said they play drums and run naked in the woods. You haven't been running naked in the woods, have you, Sam?"

"Don't be silly."

"So how long will these men's meetings last?"

Sam thought for a moment. "I think it runs until Christmas, but it might go a bit longer. It all depends on whether or not we're finished. We still have cars and baseball and hunting to talk about."

She studied him warily.

He stretched and yawned. "Well, I think I'll head off to bed. All that talk about riding mowers has worn me out."

Barbara sat at the kitchen table a while longer, too distracted to finish her crossword puzzle for wondering what Sam was really doing on Wednesday nights. She'd talked to Uly Grant's wife, Karen, about it that day at the grocery store.

"How long have you been married?" Karen had asked Barbara.

"Almost seventeen years."

"Well, there you go. That's when it starts. He's cheating on you."

A wave of nauseous fear swelled through Barbara.

"Cheating? Sam wouldn't cheat on me. He wouldn't do that."

"Well, all I know is that if Uly was going out every Wednesday night and giving me some cockamamie excuse, I'd be hiring me a detective."

Barbara had been in knots ever since.

She walked up the stairs to their bedroom. Sam was brushing his teeth, and his clothes were piled in a heap on the bedroom floor. She picked up his shirt to put it in the dirty-clothes hamper and caught a whiff of an unfamiliar odor. It wasn't unpleasant, just different. She held his shirt to her nose and sniffed. Yes, there it was. Perfume. Her heart sank. In the bathroom, Sam shut off the water and placed his toothbrush in the cup beside the sink. She stuffed his clothes in the hamper, barely able to speak for fear she might burst into tears.

As they passed, Sam reached out to hug her, but she scooted around him. "Have to use the bathroom," she mumbled, averting her eyes.

She closed the door behind her, brushed her teeth, then sat for a while, composing herself. When she came into their bedroom, Sam's bedside light was turned off and he was asleep. She stood over him, torn between anger and sorrow. She contemplated smothering him with a pillow. Get twelve women on the jury, tell her side of the story, and she'd walk away scot-free. But her better nature won out and she lay down, scrunched as far to her side as she could get without falling off, wondering how to find a detective, then drifting off into a fitful sleep.

When she wakened the next morning, she resolved to hold her head high. No man was going to ruin her life. She fixed breakfast for their sons, Levi and Addison, pointed to the pantry when Sam asked where his breakfast was, then got the boys out the door and off to school.

"Will you be home tonight?" she asked Sam when they were alone.

He walked over to the refrigerator and peered at the calendar the church had given them the year before. *The Beauty of God's Creation* calendar. Scenes from nature complete with scriptural citations, which, by the end of the year, were designed to bring even the most callous soul to the Lord.

"Not one meeting," he said. "Looks like I'll be home

tonight. Hey, I have an idea. Let's take the boys and drive over to the Hungry Rancher in Cartersburg for supper. We haven't eaten out in a long time. How about it?"

"Sure, if that's what you want."

"It's a date then."

His day passed quickly. Dale Hinshaw, their church's guardian of orthodoxy, stopped by to discuss his plans for the church's progressive Nativity scene. Then Fern Hampton came past to tell Sam his ministry to the Friendly Women's Circle had been lacking, but that he could make it up to them by bringing a devotional to their next meeting.

"When is your next meeting?" Sam asked.

"Tonight."

"Sorry, can't do it. I promised my wife and kids I'd take them out to dinner."

"Sam, this is exactly what I was talking about. You never make time for the Circle."

"I'm sorry, Fern, but I'm already committed. The next time you might not wait until the day you need me to ask."

"Jessie Peacock was supposed to bring the devotional, but she's down with the flu. I guess expecting our minister to help was just too much," Fern snapped.

"Maybe Frank could speak to the Circle," Sam suggested.

Frank was Sam's secretary. Seventy-six years old, Frank was a force of nature.

Sam walked to his office door and opened it. "Hey, Frank. Would you like to bring the devotion to tonight's meeting of the Friendly Women's Circle?"

"Sure, I'd be happy to set 'em straight."

Fern frowned. "Well, I don't know . . ." She paused for a moment, then shrugged. "I guess I don't have a choice, seeing as how our minister will be off gallivanting all over town."

"It's a deal, then. Frank with the Friendly Women, and me with my family," Sam said, stepping aside as Fern exited his office. "We're glad to be of service and you're welcome."

"Thank you, I suppose."

Sam dabbled on his sermon, then left his office at three o'clock, pausing to wish Frank luck. "If you want, I can say a prayer for the Lord to protect you."

"Thanks, but no. I'll be fine."

"What are you going to talk about?"

"I'll probably tell them a war story. That always makes the ladies swoon."

"Don't get too carried away. I don't want rumors floating around about my secretary and his wanton ways."

"Should have thought of that before you hired a stud muffin," Frank said.

"On that note, I'm leaving," Sam said. "See you tomorrow, Frank."

It was windy outside; the first of the leaves were down and skittering across the sidewalk, coming to rest in a nook of the meetinghouse. Sam walked the three blocks home, arriving just as his sons got home from school. Two hours later, they piled in the car and drove the back roads to the Hungry Rancher restaurant, where Barbara ordered a vegetable plate and Sam ordered a gargantuan steak.

He pushed back from the table, full as a blood-swelled tick, then let out a contented sigh.

"Hello, Sam," a voice behind him said.

A fellow scrapbooker was seated at the next table, an attractive young woman whose name escaped him at the moment. He smiled and gave a general greeting, a skill honed from years in the ministry. They exchanged pleasantries, and then she rose to leave. "See you next Wednesday," she said, patting him on the back, then gathering her coat and leaving.

Barbara didn't talk much on the way home, despite Sam's efforts to engage her in conversation. When they reached home, Sam checked their answering machine. Eight new messages in the space of two hours. *Looks like someone died,* he thought worriedly. He pushed the play button. The first message was from his mother, a devoted member of the Friendly Women's Circle.

"Just calling to warn you, son. Frank talked about being in the Korean War tonight at our meeting. But, uh, he digressed a bit and talked about a woman he'd met who was quite popular with the other soldiers and, well, I don't quite know how to say this, but it probably wasn't an appropriate topic for the Circle, and Fern Hampton got upset and told everyone that you'd put Frank up to it, and some of the ladies are pretty mad. Just thought you oughta know. Have a nice evening, son."

Fat chance of that.

He listened to the next seven messages, all of them from irate Friendly Women except the last one, which was from Frank. "Uh, say there, Sam, umm, you might want to give me a call when you get in."

And on that cheerful note Sam Gardner's day drew to a close.

TWO

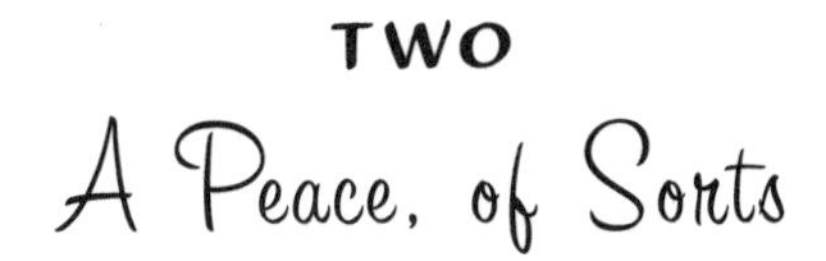

A Peace, of Sorts

Mrs. Hilda Gruber studied Sam's scrapbook with a disdainful air. "Are these all the pictures you have? This won't fill up half your scrapbook."

"Maybe if I made the letters bigger, it would take up more space and I wouldn't need as many pictures," Sam suggested.

"Scrapbook letters should be exactly one inch," she sniffed. "Of course, some scrapbookers will tell you letter size isn't important, but that's what's wrong with this world.

People make up their own rules and look where it's gotten us. Anarchy and chaos. One inch letters, Mr. Gardner. No smaller, no larger."

"Yes, ma'am. One inch. I understand."

"And some of these photographs are curled. How do you store them?"

"In a shoe box."

"You store your photographs in a shoe box?" Mrs. Gruber asked incredulously.

"Doesn't everyone?"

"I don't."

Of course you wouldn't, Sam thought.

"Class, may I have your attention," Mrs. Gruber said, tapping her ruler on Sam's desk. "I've just been informed that Mr. Gardner stores his photographs in a shoe box."

The women frowned, clearly not surprised by this sordid revelation.

"I file mine chronologically and can cross-reference them both alphabetically and by subject matter," Mrs. Gruber said proudly.

Sam's classmates applauded.

She turned to the next page in Sam's scrapbook and lifted it up for the students to view. "Dreadful. Perfectly dreadful.

No consistent theme. No thought given to balance and proportion. No obvious system of arrangement. Mr. Gardner, this scrapbook is an assault to the senses. This is nothing short of pictorial pandemonium."

She closed the scrapbook. "I don't want you to paste one more photograph in this book. Do you understand me? Not one more picture!"

"What will I do?"

"We have several students who show some promise. I want you to examine their scrapbooks. Perhaps it will inspire you."

"Yes, ma'am."

The rest of the evening passed with agonizing slowness.

He arrived home a little before ten. The house was dark, and Barbara and the boys were asleep in bed. On the drive home, he'd had an idea, and he now went to the phone to call his mother-in-law.

"Sorry to call so late, but I don't want Barbara to hear me," he explained when she answered the phone. After swearing her to secrecy, he told her about the scrapbook he was making. "Could you sort through your old pictures and send me a dozen or so pictures of Barbara when she was little? You'll need to send them to the meetinghouse so

Barbara doesn't find them. Don't put your name on the package. I have a nosy secretary."

Upstairs, Barbara had awakened to hear the tail end of Sam's conversation. She rose from their bed, flipped on the hallway light, and began descending the stairs.

"I can't talk now. She might hear us," she heard Sam say. Then he hung up the phone.

"What will I hear?" Barbara said, standing on the bottom stair and studying him.

"Oh, nothing."

"How was your men's meeting?" she asked.

"Pretty good. We talked about motorcycles."

"Motorcycles, eh?"

"Any phone calls for me?"

"Just Fern Hampton. She said, and I quote, 'If that husband of yours doesn't fire Frank by the end of the week, I will.'"

Sam grimaced.

This he did not need. In addition to being publicly humiliated by his Nazi scrapbook teacher, Sam had to deal with Dale Hinshaw, who had stopped by the meetinghouse that day to inform him he'd secured a new sponsor for that year's progressive Nativity scene.

"And who would that be?" Sam had asked.

"Bud's Mattress City over in Amo. Thing is, Bud wants to put one of their mattresses in the manger along with a sign, which I told them would be no problem."

Sam groaned inwardly.

"Yep," Dale went on, oblivious to Sam's dismay. "Uly Grant said we could put the infant Jesus in his yard and Mary and Joseph are going to be in Bea Majors's yard again, the wise men at Mabel Morrison's, the shepherds at my house, and we'll end with the heavenly hosts here at the meeting-house with hot chocolate and cookies."

He thought of telling Barbara the latest progressive Nativity developments, but decided not to bring the matter up. The pain was still too fresh. Instead, they went upstairs and went to bed. Sam fell asleep promptly, while Barbara lay awake, wondering what Sam had really done that night and whom he'd done it with.

The following days passed quickly. Sam took Monday off and Tuesday arrived at his office to find a package from his mother-in-law.

"Came in yesterday's mail," Frank said. It had taken all his willpower not to open it. "What is it?"

"None of your business," Sam told him.

"Are you still sore at me?"

"No," Sam sighed. "I'm not mad. I just wished you had been a bit more circumspect with the Friendly Women."

"All I did was talk about this woman a bunch of us guys knew about while we were in Korea. Boy, Sam, I tell you, she could—"

"Stop right there, Frank." He looked at Frank for a long moment. "What you need to do is get married."

Frank had been a widower for six years and the stress of celibacy was beginning to show.

"You know, Fern Hampton has never been married," Sam hinted.

"I'd sooner be dead."

"Can't fault you there." Sam paused. "Fern wants me to fire you."

"Yeah, I heard. So are you going to?"

"Of course not. But perhaps you ought to take a vacation for a week or two. Maybe drive down to North Carolina and visit those granddaughters."

"Hmm, probably not a bad idea," Frank said. "Maybe I'll go down for Thanksgiving."

"I was thinking maybe tomorrow. You know what they say, 'Out of sight, out of mind.' Let Fern cool down. Then when you come home, she'll be agitated about something else and will have forgotten all about it."

Sam walked into his office, with Frank right behind him. "You gonna open that envelope anytime soon?"

"I thought I might." He reached for the pocketknife he kept in his desk to open mail with, slit the end, and pulled the photographs from the envelope. He began thumbing through them one at a time while Frank peered over his shoulder.

Frank chuckled. "Cute little thing, wasn't she? Look at that. Holding a doll and packing heat at the same time."

"I think her father wanted a son," Sam said.

"So what are you doing with those pictures?"

Sam hesitated. "Promise not to tell?"

"Scout's honor."

"I'm making Barbara a picture scrapbook for her Christmas present."

He didn't mention enrolling in the class. Being the only man in a scrapbooking class was still a bit embarrassing.

Frank whistled. "Say, not a bad idea. Women love that kind of thing. Good thinking."

Sam smiled proudly. "It was a stroke of genius, if I do say so myself."

"They got classes you can take in this stuff," Frank said. "My daughter and grandkids are in one. They had to buy these special scissors and paper and tape, plus the book the pictures go in. Then there are these pens and cutouts and punches and stamps and stencils. It's cost them about four hundred dollars. They could've bought themselves a lawn mower for what they're spending on those picture books."

Sam had dropped over five hundred on his scrapbook class so far, but wasn't about to tell that to Frank.

Coincidentally, at that very moment, Barbara Gardner was studying the bank statement that had arrived in the morning mail, noting a pattern of withdrawals over the past several months. That's odd, she thought. Wonder what that's all about? She suspected the worst. Sam's probably wining and dining some chippy, she said to herself.

She picked up the phone and dialed the meetinghouse number.

"I'll get that," Frank said, reaching for the phone. "Hello."

"Hey, Frank. Is Sam there?"

"It's your wife," he said, handing Sam the phone.

Sam listened for a moment, then said, "Withdrawals, you say. Gee, let me think. Yes, maybe I did make those." He paused while she spoke. "Oh, you know, this and that. First one thing and then another. Nothing special. Just needed to pick up a few things."

"Five hundred dollars worth?!" Barbara said, in such a loud voice Frank could hear her across the room. He winced, then backed out of Sam's office, closing the door behind him.

Sam came out a few moments later, walking with a slight stagger, his hair laid back as if he'd encountered a hurricane. "Boy, is she mad. I tell you, Frank, Christmas is getting more dangerous every year."

"I hope your marriage makes it until then," Frank said. "It'd be a shame for you to put all this work into a scrapbook for your wife, only to have her leave you."

"Six more weeks. If I can make it six more weeks, I'm home free." He stumbled back into his office and collapsed in his chair with a moan. "What was I thinking? Why didn't I just get her some pot holders? She was saying just the other day she needed new pot holders."

"Can't go wrong with pot holders," Frank agreed.

"But no, I had to be creative. I had to get her the perfect Christmas gift. Now look where it's gotten me. My wife hates my guts."

"Maybe you ought to come to North Carolina with me," Frank suggested. "Let your wife cool down. You know what they say, 'Out of sight, out of mind.'"

Sam sighed. "I wanted to surprise her with the scrapbook, but now I think maybe I oughta go ahead and tell her. I don't want her to think I'm having an affair."

"Well, you do what you want," Frank said. "But I wouldn't knuckle under if it was me."

"What do you mean? I'm not knuckling under. I'm just going to let her know what I'm doing so she doesn't worry."

"And spoil your surprise? Sam, you'll ruin the whole thing. You know you're not having an affair, so she's got nothing to worry about. Besides, think how fun it'll be on Christmas morning when you show it to her. And now you're gonna tell her, just because you're afraid of her?"

"I am not afraid of my wife."

"Then don't tell her."

"I thought you were going to North Carolina," Sam grumbled.

The rest of the day passed at a crawl. Sam was tormented, unsure whether or not to tell Barbara what he'd been doing.

When he walked in the door in the late afternoon, Barbara was in the kitchen, cooking supper. He slipped up behind her and put his arms around her. "Hey, honey."

"Hi, Sam."

"What's for dinner?" he asked, sniffing the air.

"Beef stew."

"Mmm."

"Sam, can we talk?" Barbara asked, shutting off the flame underneath the stew and turning to face him.

"Sure. What you want to talk about?"

"About what you're doing on Wednesday nights."

Sam hesitated. "There are some things I can't talk about right now, but I want you to know I love you and would never do anything to betray your trust."

She sagged in his arms and began to weep. "Oh, Sam. I've been so worried about you. I heard you on the phone the other evening talking with somebody. You've been gone all these nights. And then finding that money gone from our savings account, well, I was just worried sick. I want you to be honest with me."

"I would never be unfaithful," Sam promised. "I thought you knew that." He kissed away a lone tear on her cheek.

"I don't know what I was thinking. You just hear so many stories these days of spouses cheating on one another."

"We don't do that," Sam said firmly. "Understood?"

"Understood," she said.

And standing in the kitchen, they made their peace, the pleasant scent of beef stew wafting through the air as the weight of worry fell away.

THREE

Hair Today, Gone Tomorrow

Thanksgiving Day came and went, hurtling past before the Gardners could scarcely draw a breath. The day after Thanksgiving the Christmas shopping season began in earnest at Kivett's Five and Dime, which is where Barbara Gardner bumped into Karen Grant in the toy aisle.

"So how's that husband of yours? Still going to that men's group?" Karen asked, with a slight snicker.

"I'm not sure what he's doing," Barbara said. "But whatever he's doing, I know it's nothing bad."

"Well, I hope you're right." She paused for a thoughtful moment. "Do you get *Midwest Romance* magazine?"

"No."

"Well, I was reading in this month's issue about a man who was gone from his house once a week and his wife thought he was cheating, but it turns out he had this weird disease and was being treated and didn't want his wife to know. By the time his wife found out the truth, he was dead."

Her chin trembled as she told it, clearly moved by this story of silent and selfless suffering. "Isn't that positively romantic?"

"Thank you for cheering me up, Karen. You can't imagine my comfort in knowing that my husband isn't cheating on me because he's too busy dying. But I assure you, if Sam were sick, I'd know about it. He gets a cold and he acts like the world has come to an end."

"Don't they all," said Karen, patting Barbara on the hand. "Well, I have to finish this shopping. You take care."

"You too."

Barbara was organized to the hilt and a whiz at shopping. Within an hour, she was tucking the sacks into the trunk of the car and heading home to hide the packages before

Sam and the boys returned home from their annual after-Thanksgiving hike in Miriam and Ellis Hodge's woodlot.

She hid their presents underneath a floorboard in the attic. Mrs. Neely, who'd owned the house before them, had told Barbara about the hiding places in the house, the loose floorboard underneath the attic window being one and a false wall in the master bedroom closet being the other. Sam had found the one in their closet, but despite his best efforts to find his Christmas presents, hadn't yet discovered the loose floorboard.

She scooted aside a box of Christmas decorations and pried up the board, fitting the presents in between the floor joists. Perfect. Sam would never find them.

That Saturday passed quickly, spent raking the last of the fallen oak leaves and burning them at the curb. The next day at church marked the unofficial start of Christmas. Sam had labored, ever since he had began pastoring there six years before, to get the church to follow the liturgical calendar. He'd brought it up again at the November elders meeting.

"So what exactly does that mean?" Fern Hampton had asked.

"Well, Fern," Sam had explained, "it means we don't sing Christmas songs until Christmas Day. On the Sundays leading up to Christmas, we sing Advent songs."

"What's an Advent song?"

"You know, songs like 'Come, Thou Long-Expected Jesus' and 'Let All Mortal Flesh Keep Silence,'" Sam suggested.

"Never heard of them. Besides, it'll never work," Fern had said immediately. "You tell Bea Majors we can't sing Christmas songs until Christmas and she'll quit. Then we'll have to find ourselves a new organist."

The Elders Committee of Harmony Friends Meeting, though basically competent, would never be confused for the world's greatest deliberative body. Sam let it drop.

He took Monday off and Tuesday was back in his office, filling out the year-end statistical report he had to mail off to the Quaker headquarters in the city. Three births, four deaths, two membership transfers out, and three membership transfers in.

"Looks like we came out even," he told Frank.

"How'd we come out money-wise?" Frank asked.

"I'm not doing the financial report. Deena Morrison is. But I think with the bequest from Ethel Mayhew's estate, we'll be in the black. By several thousand dollars from the looks of it."

"Then this might be a good time for me to ask for a raise," Frank said. "Who do I need to see about that?"

Sam leaned back in his chair and thought for a moment.

"Well, let me see. This year Fern Hampton has oversight of pastoral and staff matters, so you'd need to talk with her."

"There goes my raise."

"Probably so."

Wednesday afternoon found Sam leaving early for his scrapbooking class. If he was to finish it in time for Christmas, he'd have to work long hours. At Mrs. Gruber's insistence, he'd started over, undoing what had already cost him a small fortune. She'd been pleased at his idea to include pictures from Barbara's childhood and, though not effusive in her praise, had refrained from publicly castigating him. This, for Sam, was real progress.

Buoyed by her modest support, Sam pulled a new sheet of display paper from his folder and arranged several pictures on the page, taping them into place. He punched out the letters *MY CHILDHOOD* and began gluing them on the sheet, arranging them just so. One-inch-high letters, just as Mrs. Gruber had taught him. She stood watching him, peering over his shoulder, every now and then nodding her approval. Occasionally, a fellow student walked by and surveyed his work, impressed by his progress.

Sam pulled a photograph from his briefcase and showed it to Mrs. Gruber. "Look, this is my wife's first-grade class.

There she is right there," he said, pointing to a thin, pale girl with a missing front tooth and pigtails.

"Very nice touch," Mrs. Gruber said softly, before she realized what she was doing, then blushed from her naked display of kindness.

The other students were noticeably warmer toward him. One woman even loaned him her wavy-edged scissors and during their break held a lengthy conversation with him about the merits of Super Glue versus glue sticks.

"I'm a Super Glue man myself," Sam said. "Sure, it's a bit risky, but things stay put. Oh, I tried the glue stick, but the pictures slid too much."

"Does Mrs. Gruber know you use Super Glue?" the woman asked.

"Does she know! She's the one who suggested it," Sam said, thrilled at his newfound status as an up-and-coming gluer.

He leaned back in his chair and sipped his coffee, trying to remain humble but succeeding only with great difficulty.

"If you want, I'll share my stickers with you," the woman said.

"Thank you," Sam said. "But I prefer to paint my designs."

The woman looked at him, clearly impressed, and then sighed. "Your wife sure is lucky to have you. The only thing my husband does is watch NASCAR races. He'd never join a scrapbooking class."

Sam smiled modestly. "I've always had a deep appreciation for the arts."

It has been noted by wise persons of old that pride goeth before a fall, and regrettably this ancient proverb proved true. While Sam was gluing the second *D* in *CHILDHOOD,* the bottom of his Super Glue tube gave out and the glue leaked in a puddle on his desk. He wiped it up with paper towels, managing in the process to cover his hands with Super Glue, which, in a moment of frustration, he transferred to his hair while he was brushing a strand off his forehead.

Sitting there, he was transported back to fourth grade, the last time he'd inadvertently glued his hand to his head. He tugged on his hair, but was unable to free his hand. In desperation, he grabbed an even larger lock of hair and tugged more fiercely, only worsening the situation. Now he had an entire fistful of hair bonded to his hand. He reached up with his other hand, instinctively, to pry his fingers loose and multiplied his predicament when it too became stuck.

To his left he heard a chuckle, followed by a titter to his right, and before long everyone in the class was reveling in his fall from lofty scrapbooking heights.

"Sam Gardner, stop this nonsense now," Mrs. Hilda Gruber said, with a wag of her finger.

"I can't help myself. My tube of glue broke."

She let out an exasperated sigh. "Didn't I tell you to be careful? I distinctly remember saying that, although Super Glue is a superior adhesive, it poses certain challenges and would require your full attention. Do you remember my telling you that?"

"Yes, ma'am."

She turned to the woman seated next to Sam. "Scissors, please."

"You're not going to stab me, are you?" Sam asked.

"Though I am sorely tempted, no, I will not stab you. I'm going to cut your hair away from your hand."

"Hands."

"Yes, your hands. You've managed to make quite a mess, Mr. Gardner. And I was starting to have hopes for you."

She began hacking away indiscriminately at Sam's hair with the wavy-edged scissors. Thick clumps of hair fell to the floor and soon his hands were freed. Hilda Gruber lectured him all the while, ending with a firm pronouncement that he was being demoted to glue sticks.

His hands were still stuck in fists, from which wisps of hair protruded. "How do I get my hands open?"

The woman next to him spoke. "When my son glued himself with Super Glue, I had to take him to the hospital to get it off."

Sam frowned, then strained to open his hands, without success. He went to the rest room and began scrubbing fiercely; finally he could open his hands, though not without the loss of several layers of skin. Finished with his hands, he glanced at himself in the mirror and was horrified to see large patches of hair missing. He appeared to have fallen prey to a mowing scythe.

His scrapbooking ardor cooled, he returned to the classroom, stored his supplies in the closet, and drove home. Passing down Main Street, he noticed Kyle Weathers exiting his barbershop. He pulled up to the curb.

Kyle looked at his hair. "My gosh, man, what happened to you?"

"I'd rather not say. Can you fix it?"

Kyle studied the top of Sam's head. "I can't make any promises. But if I give you a buzz cut, I think we can make it look all right."

Sam sighed. "Okay, then. Let's get it done."

It took Kyle fifteen minutes to shear Sam's head. He followed up with a neck shave and, because it was close to Christmas and he was in a charitable mood, threw in a nose-hair trim for free. He loosened the apron from around Sam's neck and brushed him off. Sam ran his still tender hand across his scalp, which now resembled a shoe brush.

"Sure you don't want to tell me what happened?" Kyle asked.

"Never in my life have I been more sure of anything," Sam said.

He walked out to his car feeling several pounds lighter. It was curious how heavy hair could be.

When he reached home, the boys were in bed. Barbara was in the kitchen finishing the supper dishes. She looked up as Sam came through the door, then her face paled. He's balder than a cue ball, she thought. My Lord, he has cancer!

"What happened, Sam?" she asked, her voice shaking.

"I'd rather not talk about it."

His reticence confirmed her worst suspicions. He was dying and couldn't bear the thought of telling her. She went to his side and embraced him, rubbing her hand over his stubbly head. "You can tell. You can tell me anything."

"Not this I can't. At least not yet. I'm not ready for you to know. In time, you'll find out."

She was overcome with shame for suspecting him of having an affair. All these months he'd been bearing this terrible burden alone, unwilling to saddle her and their children with the tragic news of his affliction.

She clung to him and began to weep.

"It's just my hair, honey. It'll grow back."

He's so brave, she marveled to herself.

"When do you think you'll be able to tell me?" she asked.

"I want to get us through Christmas," he said. "Then we can talk about it."

He doesn't want to spoil the children's Christmas, she thought. Such a wonderful husband and father.

As for Sam, he couldn't believe Barbara's change of spirit. She couldn't do enough for him. She served him hot chocolate while he sat in his easy chair, then drew a tub of hot water for him, washed his back and other places he couldn't reach, then dried him off.

"I like your hair," she said, rubbing a towel over it. She glanced at the towel and was alarmed to notice pieces of hair on it. She wiped his neck and he sighed contentedly. It felt wonderful to get those itchy remnants of his haircut off his neck and head.

They made their way into their bedroom, where they lay together, side by side.

"Would you like a back rub?" she asked.

"Sure," he said, thoroughly mystified by her tender care, but enjoying it immensely.

He rolled over onto his stomach and she began kneading his back gently. He sighed contentedly.

"Does it hurt much?" she asked, almost afraid to hear the answer.

"Only when Kyle pokes the scissors in my ear," Sam said.

Dying of cancer and he still has a sense of humor, Barbara thought. What a brave man he is.

And so Sam's otherwise difficult day drew to a close in the warm embrace of his wife, whom he loved deeply, but seldom understood.

FOUR
The Secret Gets Out

The first week of December found Ray from the street department leaning precariously from a ladder while hanging a strand of Christmas bulbs from the marquee of the Royal Theater across the street to Grant's Hardware, then back across Washington Street to Owen Stout's law office. Kyle Weathers and a clutch of old men were watching from the barbershop, placing bets on whether this would be the year Ray fell from his ladder to a sure and certain death.

Sam Gardner walked past, careful not to cross under the ladder and usher all manner of bad luck into his life. He paused to watch Ray secure the lights to an iron hook over Owen Stout's window.

"How's the weather up there?" Sam asked.

Ray, never one for conversation, grunted.

"Been nice talking to you," Sam said, walking on.

"Yep."

He walked past the barbershop, looked through the window, and waved.

"Boy, you sure did a number on his head," Stanley Farlow said to Kyle Weathers. "I haven't seen a haircut like that since I was in the army. How'd you cut it so close without drawing blood?"

"Practice," Kyle said proudly. "You know my motto. Every haircut a walking testimony."

Sam continued on, pausing to view the Christmas display in the window of the Rexall drugstore. Thad Cramer, the pharmacist, was arranging magazines on the shelf beside the counter. He'd owned the Rexall since Sam was a boy and would sneak peeks at the *Police Gazette.* He still felt guilty whenever he saw Thad, so he hurried along the sidewalk toward the meetinghouse.

Overhead, the sky was a scuddy gray. The morning radio had predicted the first snowfall of the season, and Sam had spent a good part of the morning hunting his rubber boots, which he'd finally found in the basement behind a box of canning jars. He used his search for the boots as an excuse to nose around for his Christmas presents, but had come up dry.

Frank was seated at his desk, reading a book.

"Morning, Frank."

"Hey, Sam."

"Say, Frank, how's the December newsletter coming along?"

"Not done yet."

Sam sighed. "You know, other churches send out their newsletter before the month actually gets here. That way if there's a church event early in the month, people know about it in time. I hate interfering with your reading, but do you think maybe you could finish the newsletter today?"

"Probably not," Frank said. "I'm on strike until I get a raise."

"What do you mean, you're on strike? You hardly do anything as it is."

"Insult me all you wish. It will not lessen my commitment to justice in the workplace. See my button." He lowered his book. Pinned to his checkered flannel shirt was a large red button that read *Workers of the World, Unite!*

"Oh, brother."

"We're all on strike."

"We? Who's we?"

"Donna Lefter, the secretary at the Baptist church, and Sister Rosalie over at the Catholic church, and Harriet Combs at the Methodist church."

Sam shook his head in disgust. "Frank, I don't have the time for this nonsense. It's three weeks from Christmas, and we have a lot of work to do."

Sam started to walk into his office.

"You wouldn't cross a picket line, would you, Sam?"

"What picket line? I don't see a picket line."

Frank pointed to a line of masking tape fixed to the floor at the entrance to Sam's office. "All we want is an extra fifty dollars a month and another coffee break. We want new photocopiers too. Ours are all junk."

"I can't believe this," Sam said, clearly exasperated. "Who's gonna finish this newsletter? I don't have time. I'll have to bring in some extra help."

"Scabs! You'd bring in scabs? You're not going to be a

union buster, are you, Sam? I thought Quakers were on the side of the poor and the oppressed."

"Well," Sam said weakly, "I suppose we are. Can I least go in my office and call Miriam Hodge?"

Miriam Hodge was the head elder of Harmony Friends Meeting.

"Go ahead. It was her idea anyway."

"What was her idea?"

"My going on strike," Frank said, leaning back in his chair and grinning. "I told her I needed a raise, and she said she didn't think we had the money, and I asked her what could be done, and she said, 'Well, Frank, I suppose you could always go on strike.' So here I am."

Sam went into his office, pulling the door closed behind him. He emerged several minutes later. "Okay, it's a deal. I've spoken with Miriam, and she thinks we can come up with fifty dollars extra a month and another coffee break."

"Are you serious?"

"You bet, Frank. You deserve it."

"Sam, I don't know what to say. I really appreciate it. Thank you."

"Don't thank me. Thank Brother Norman."

"Brother Norman? Why him?"

"The Friendly Women are going to pay for your raise out of Brother Norman's shoe fund."

Since time immemorial, the Friendly Women's Circle had been the big money behind Brother Norman's shoe ministry to the Choctaw Indians, through which hundreds of Choctaw feet had been shod over the years.

"Isn't that nice of them?" Sam continued. "Of course, that means some Choctaw children won't have shoes this winter, but you deserve a raise."

"Darn tootin'," said Frank. "Besides it'll be good for them. Toughens 'em up."

Sam frowned. This conversation wasn't taking the turn he'd anticipated.

"You're a cold man, Frank."

Frank stared straight ahead, still as a Choctaw Indian.

Sam glanced at his watch. "Well, I must say I'm a little disappointed in you. I'd like to stay and discuss this with you further, but I have a Library Board meeting."

When Sam left, Frank picked up the phone and dialed Donna Lefter at the Baptist church. "So how'd it go with you. Did you get your raise?"

"The pastor's going to talk with the deacons," she said.

"You won't believe what Sam did. He told me he was going to talk to Miriam Hodge about giving me a raise. So he goes in his office to call her and comes out and says they can give me a raise, but it'll have to come out of the shoe fund for the Choctaw Indian children. Thing is, I know for a fact Miriam's not home today. She's at her sister's house in the city. He was trying to make me feel guilty. It was all I could do to keep a straight face."

Donna Lefter hooted over the phone. "Boy, for a pastor, he sure is sneaky."

"Not sneaky enough, though."

"So are you really going to go on strike?"

"Of course not. I'm just pulling his chain. I would like a raise, though. Been here six years, and I've not had a raise in all that time. And the longer I'm here, the more stuff they give me to do. Now Sam's working only half a day on Wednesdays, and the work's backing up. Guess I'll stay over today and get it all done."

"Why's he taking Wednesdays off?" Donna Lefter asked.

"He told me he's going to some men's group, whatever it is they do."

Donna Lefter chuckled. "What is it about pastors anyway? They always have to belong to some kind of support group."

"I tell you who needs a support group," Frank said. "Church secretaries, that's who!"

"You got that right, mister."

"Then again, even if we did have one, we wouldn't have time to go."

"Amen to that," Donna said.

"Take care."

"Bye, Frank."

Frank busied himself for the next several hours typing and duplicating the newsletter. He pasted the labels on, licked one hundred and fifty-three stamps, and affixed them to the newsletters, which he carried two blocks to the post office. Then he went home, gargled to get the glue taste out of his mouth, and soaked his feet.

While Frank was perched on a kitchen chair, steeping in Epsom salts, Sam was headed through the country to his scrapbooking class in Cartersburg. He had three more sessions before the class ended for Christmas break, and he was nowhere near done. At this rate, he'd have to either scale back his plans or hire it done.

He arrived early. Mrs. Hilda Gruber was seated at her desk, anticipating his arrival, her metal-edged, knuckle-rapping ruler within easy reach.

Sam's star had taken a considerable fall after his Super Glue accident, and Mrs. Gruber was in no mood to coddle him.

She opened the closet so he could retrieve his materials, then frisked him to make sure he wasn't carrying a tube of Super Glue.

"Sit down," she said, pointing to a seat.

He took a seat, hardly able to look Hilda Gruber in the face, so deep was his shame.

She rose from her chair, walked around her desk, and stood in front of Sam, looming over him.

"You're a deep disappointment to me," she said, rapping her ruler on Sam's desk for added emphasis, tapping out each word. "I had such hopes for you when you showed me your wife's childhood pictures. I thought you were starting to understand what it meant to be a scrapbooker. Now look at you. Glue splotches on your scrapbook. Your hair's a sight. You've fallen behind. Can you give me one good reason why I shouldn't flunk you?"

Sam thought back over his brief career as a scrapbooker, how he'd lurched from one disaster to another. "I guess not."

"It's simply too dangerous having you around. We took a vote after you left last time and think it's best that you gather your things and leave," Hilda Gruber said, with a tap of her ruler.

"Now?"

"Now!"

Sam sagged inside himself. There went his wife's Christmas present. Looks like I'm back to giving her pot holders, he thought.

He placed his belongings in a paper sack and shuffled out the door before the others arrived. It was a long drive back home, and by the time he pulled in the driveway he was thoroughly despondent.

Barbara cooked his favorite supper to boost his spirits, but it had little effect. After supper, he watched the evening news, then went to bed.

Barbara, beside herself with worry, phoned Frank. After exchanging pleasantries she asked Frank if Sam had seemed different lately.

"Not too much. I mean he got his hair cut, but that's all. Why do you ask?"

Barbara hesitated. Then, unable to bear the burden alone any longer, she decided to confide in Frank.

"Has Sam told you what he's doing on Wednesday nights?"

"Just that he's going to a men's group."

"I wish that were true," Barbara said, her voice catching. "If I tell you something, you have to promise you won't say anything to him or anyone else."

"Of course I won't. What's going on?"

"I think Sam might be really sick and that he's been getting treatment on Wednesdays and not telling us."

"Don't you think he would say something? You know Sam. If he's sick, he let's everyone know it."

"I don't think he wants to ruin Christmas for the boys," Barbara said. "I think he wants to wait until after Christmas to say anything."

Still somewhat skeptical, Frank asked, "What do you think is wrong with him?"

Barbara paused before speaking, as if speaking the word might make it come true. "I think he has cancer and that he's been getting chemotherapy and that's why his hair fell out."

"Oh, Lord. That's terrible." Frank fell quiet and didn't say a word for several moments.

"Are you still there?" Barbara asked.

"Yes. I just feel horrible about this. I played a joke on him today. I told him I was on strike and that I wouldn't be doing any more work until I got a raise, and when he left the meetinghouse he was all agitated. I had no idea."

"We have to watch out for him," Barbara said. "Don't let him work too hard. Okay, Frank?"

"You got it."

Frank thought for a moment. "Do you get *Midwest Romance* magazine?"

"No."

"Well, I was reading it the other day, and it had this story about this man who had this weird disease and he—"

"I know, he died. Karen Grant told me."

"What I mean is that maybe Sam doesn't have cancer. Maybe it's something else and they'll cure it. Maybe he's got one of those diseases that you get from being bit by a mouse and they're giving him antibiotics or something once a week."

"Oh, I hope that's it. I don't know what I'd do without him."

"He's gonna make it, Barbara. Don't give up hope."

"Thank you, Frank," she said quietly, then hung up the phone.

Having told Frank, she felt better for sharing the weight of worry and busied herself washing the supper dishes, which served as a helpful distraction. Then she took her bath, slipped into her nightgown, went to bed, and fell asleep, her body pressed against her hairless husband's.

FIVE

Within four days, half the town, after Frank had sworn them to secrecy, had been told of Sam's imminent demise. Without mentioning names, Bob Miles at the *Herald* had written a touching editorial about the brevity of life and the inscrutable ways of the Almighty. On Sunday morning at meeting for worship, the women dabbed their eyes and hugged him; the men patted him on the back and raved about his sermon, which Sam hadn't spent that much time preparing for worrying about his scrapbook. It had been a stream-of-consciousness sermon, with a lot of *On the one hand, this . . . but on the other hand, that*'s punctuating his remarks.

"Wonderful message," Asa Peacock had told him, pumping Sam's arm like a thirsty man priming a well. "Don't remember when I've heard such fine preaching."

"Unusually perceptive," Miriam Hodge noted when she came through the line after worship to shake Sam's hand.

Even Fern Hampton allowed that it had been one of his better efforts.

On Monday morning he woke up filled with energy and more than a little angry at having flunked out of a scrapbooking class where grades weren't even given.

He turned to Barbara. "By golly, I'm not going to take this sitting down."

"That's the spirit," she said. "You can whip this!"

"Darn tootin'," he said.

In the six years Frank had been his secretary, Sam's vocabulary had expanded to include a number of sayings—"Darn tootin'," "Goldarnit," "Jumpin' Jehosaphat!" and "Yessiree bob."

He ate a hearty breakfast. It pleased Barbara immensely to note his vigorous appetite.

I'll show that Hilda Gruber, he thought, while walking to

his office. I'll make the finest scrapbook this world has ever seen! He clenched his jaw, determined to overcome this grave injustice.

He strode into his office, and Frank leaped to his feet. Frank's strike had been short-lived. Indeed, since last Thursday he'd been unusually solicitous.

"Let me get you some coffee, Sam."

"Thank you, Frank, but no. I don't have time to drink coffee."

He set his briefcase on his desk and pulled his scrapbook from it, arranging it on his desk.

"Is that the scrapbook you're making for Barbara?"

"Yep."

Frank marveled silently at Sam's dedication. Dying of some fearsome disease and all he cared about was his wife's Christmas present.

Sam glanced at his watch, at the tiny date in the three o'clock window. "I have fourteen days to finish this scrapbook, and I'm going to do it if it kills me."

Frank winced at Sam's choice of words.

He stood behind Sam, scrutinizing his scrapbook. "Mind a bit of advice?"

"About what?"

"Your scrapbook."

"What do you know about scrapbooks?" Sam said, with a snort.

"What do you mean, what do I know? I know plenty. What do you think I did the whole time I was in North Carolina. My daughter and granddaughters are in a scrapbooking class. It's all we did the whole time I was down there."

"So what's your advice?"

"Your lettering is all the same. You need to make it different. Be creative."

"I thought all the lettering had to be one inch high."

"Where'd you get that crazy idea?"

Sam hesitated, and not wanting to revisit his humiliating failure in the scrapbook class, said simply, "I read it somewhere."

"There's your problem, right there. You read too much. I've told you that before. Scoot over and lemme take a look at this mess."

Frank wheeled his chair in from his office, plunked down beside Sam, and began flipping through the scrapbook. "What's this?"

Sam smiled proudly. "That's Barbara giving birth to Levi. Took that picture myself."

"And what makes you think your wife will want the entire world to see her uterus?"

Sam reddened. "I just thought since it was a special moment she'd want to have it in her scrapbook."

"Was the first night of your honeymoon special?" Frank asked.

Sam thought for a moment, smiling at the memory. "Very special."

"Well, then, you have any pictures of that we can put in here?"

"Of course not," Sam said indignantly. "Besides, that's a private matter."

"My point exactly," Frank said. "Same with the birth picture. We're all glad you have children, but we don't want to see their conception or their birth. Jumpin' Jehosaphat, Sam, what were you thinking?"

"I guess you have a point," Sam conceded, removing the picture.

By the time Frank had gone through the scrapbook, he'd removed every picture but two.

"This is going to be the world's thinnest scrapbook," Sam said glumly.

"You just don't have an eye for pictures, that's all," Frank said. "But not to worry, because I do. Where do you keep your pictures?"

"In a shoe box in our front closet."

Frank shook his head, nearly overwhelmed by the task at hand. "He keeps his pictures in a shoe box," he muttered under his breath. "Why aren't I surprised?" He turned to Sam. "Can you sneak the shoe box out of your house and get it here to the office, or do you need me to do that too?"

"I think I can sneak something from my own house," Sam said. "I'm not a total idiot."

Frank rose from his chair. "Tomorrow then. Now you'll have to excuse me. I have work to do."

He shrugged on his coat and tugged his hat down over his ears.

"Where are you going?" Sam asked.

"To the scrapbooking store in the city. You don't have half the supplies you need."

It was a five-hour round trip, which gave Frank plenty of time to stew about Sam. He worried that he'd been too hard on him, but putting up a gruff front was all that kept him from breaking down in front of Sam. Forty-four years old, two little kids, and he's dying from a mouse bite, he thought bitterly. There's no justice in this world.

He bought three hundred dollars worth of materials, money he'd been saving for a new truck. With this being Sam's last Christmas and all, it was the least he could do.

Frank arrived early the next morning and made coffee for Sam, who appeared a little after eight carrying a toolbox.

"I told Barbara I had to bring my tools to fix the toilet in the men's bathroom," he said, lifting the shoe box of pictures from his toolbox.

"Good thinking," Frank said.

They began sorting through the pictures. "First, we eliminate all the pictures that make her look fat. Women hate looking at pictures that make them look fat."

"She weighs only a hundred and thirty-five," Sam said.

"And yet just this Sunday morning she put on a skirt and asked you if it made her look fat. Didn't she?"

"How'd you know?"

"They all do that," Frank said. He studied a picture of Barbara standing beside a canoe, then set it in the keep stack. "That's a nice one," he said, tapping it with his finger.

Sam smiled. "We were on a camping trip. Before we had the boys."

"Now here she is sitting in the canoe wearing a life jacket," Frank said, picking up another picture. "Do you remember what she said when she saw that picture?"

Sam thought for a moment. "I believe she said the life jacket made her look big."

"See what I mean." He put the offending picture back in the box. "Won't be needing that one."

Frank continued to pull pictures from the shoe box. "How come you have so many pictures of her laying in bed asleep?"

"Oh, I don't know. I just think she looks cute when she's sleeping."

"Women do not like to have their picture taken when they have morning hair," Frank said. "You're lucky she didn't slap you for taking these pictures."

"So they don't go in the scrapbook either?"

"Nope," Frank said, tossing them back in the shoe box.

They worked their way through the entire box until they had a suitable batch of photographs stacked on Sam's desk.

Frank spread them out on the desk and surveyed them. "Now we have to divide them into categories."

"Well," Sam said, pointing to half a dozen different photos, "these are from her childhood, so let's put them together."

"Better yet, let's take this childhood picture of you on your bicycle and this picture of your boys at the beach and put them alongside one of Barbara's childhood pictures, and we'll call that section *The Lazy Days of Summer* and we'll put a nice summery border on that page."

"Yessiree bob," Sam said. "I like it."

It took them several hours to group the photographs, and by lunchtime they were famished. Sam had skipped breakfast and was so hungry he had a headache. "Think I'll just lay down for a few minutes and rest my eyes," he told Frank.

It was all Frank could do not to weep, seeing Sam stretched out on the couch, his body under assault by this mysterious malady.

"How about I go get us some hamburgers from the Coffee Cup?" Frank asked.

"Ketchup only, no cheese," Sam said weakly. "Say, you wouldn't have any aspirin, would you?"

"I'll stop by the Rexall and get you some, buddy. You hang in there, you hear."

Frank hurried the two blocks to the Coffee Cup and ordered their meal.

"How's Sam doing?" Vinny Toricelli, the owner of the Coffee Cup, asked Frank.

"Not good at all. He's laying down over at the church."

Vinny shook his head. "I just can't believe he's got polio. I thought they had that cured."

"He doesn't have polio. Who told you that?"

"That's what Kyle Weathers said he had."

"That's not right. I looked it up myself. He's got some kind of virus you get from mouse bites."

"I heard about that. Hey, that stuff'll kill you."

"He's in a pretty bad way," Frank said glumly.

The bell over the door rang as Asa Peacock walked in. "Hey, Frank. How's Sam?"

"Poorly."

"Danged cancer. This just makes me sick."

"He doesn't have cancer," Vinny Toricelli said. "For Pete's sake, get your facts right. He's got a mouse virus. Who told you he had cancer?"

"Fern Hampton called Jessie and told her he had cancer."

"Well, right there's your problem," Vinny said. "People are running their mouths off without knowing what they're talking about."

"How long are they givin' him?" Asa asked.

"'Til just after Christmas," Frank said. "He's making Barbara a scrapbook for her Christmas present, and I think he wants to live long enough to give it to her."

Asa and Vinny grimaced, their chins trembling with grief. Vinny wrapped the hamburgers in waxed papers and placed them in a paper sack. Frank reached for his wallet, but Vinny held up his hand. "On the house. You tell Sam we're thinking of him."

"Can't do that. I'm not supposed to know."

"Well, we're thinkin' of him all the same."

"Thanks, Vinny."

He swung past the Rexall on his way back to the meetinghouse and bought a bottle of aspirin.

"These are for Sam," he explained to Thad Cramer.

"How's he doing?"

"Pitiful. You know he lost all his hair."

Thad shook his head mournfully. "I saw him just this morning, walking by on his way to work. To be honest, I'm surprised he's still up and about."

"He's running on pure willpower. He wants to make it to Christmas so he can give Barbara a gift he's made her."

"What's that?"

Frank glanced around the Rexall. "Promise not to tell anybody?"

"Sure."

"He's makin' her a picture scrapbook. Now, don't you tell anyone. Boy, if there's one thing I can't abide, it's a gossip."

"Tick a lock," Thad said, zipping his fingers across his lips.

He paid for the aspirin and arrived back at the meeting-house to find Sam asleep on the couch. He considered not waking him and letting him have his rest, but he needed nourishment too. He shook Sam gently on the shoulder. "Wake up, buddy. I got our lunch."

He arranged two places at his desk where they could eat. Sam devoured his hamburger and ate half of Frank's, then swallowed two aspirin and within an hour was considerably revived, which gladdened Frank's heart.

But looking at Sam, with his pale scalp and the bags under his eyes, he still couldn't help but worry, and he prayed that when it came Sam's time to go, the Lord would take him quickly and without pain.

SIX
The Dread Deepens

Johnny Mackey at the Mackey Funeral Home had been planning Sam Gardner's funeral since he'd first learned of Sam's impending death two weeks before, when Frank had phoned to tell him.

"We're hopin' he'll make it through to Christmas. Probably lookin' at a funeral on the twenty-ninth or thirtieth," Frank told him, his voice catching.

Johnny was beside himself with worry, fretting how best to accommodate the flood of mourners who would mark Sam's passing. It was a week from Christmas, and he'd spent an entire morning rearranging the chairs for the anticipated crowds. He'd rolled the caskets out of their display room and into the garage to make room for additional grievers.

The Wednesday before Christmas, in the late afternoon, he drove his truck to the meetinghouse to borrow a hundred folding chairs, a delicate undertaking since he wasn't supposed to know of Sam's illness. He hoped Sam wouldn't pry, but had no such luck.

"What in the world do you need a hundred chairs for?" Sam asked.

"Uh, well, Sam, it's like this. We're having a family reunion, and it's going to be at the funeral home."

"I thought you had your family reunions in the summer at the park."

"Just wanted to do things a little different this year," Johnny Mackey said.

"Well then, help yourself."

Johnny hesitated in the doorway, looking slightly embarrassed. He cleared his throat. "Say, Sam, could you give me a hand carrying 'em out to the truck?" He felt guilty asking Sam to carry chairs for his own funeral, but when a man is pushing eighty and his knees are shot with arthritis, he doesn't have the luxury of pride.

Sam carried the chairs up from the basement four at a time, while Johnny counted them off and fiddled with his pipe.

"Eighty down, twenty to go," Johnny said, an aromatic swirl of pipe smoke whirling around his head.

On the last haul, a chair slipped from Sam's grasp and when he moved quickly to grab it, he felt something give in his back, deep in his bones, and down he went, doubled over in pain.

"Think you can get 'em the rest of the way up the stairs?" Johnny asked, looking on.

Sam dragged them up, one by one, then hobbled home past the town's citizenry, all of whom were now shocked by his precipitous decline—bald and bent and moving like Pa Kettle.

"I can't bear to look at that man," Kathy at the Kut 'n' Kurl said while coloring Karen Grant's hair. "It just breaks my heart."

"I was the one who diagnosed him," Karen said. "The exact same thing happened to a man in Dubuque. I read about it in *Midwest Romance,* and I told Barbara he was dying."

"I shook hands with him last Sunday at church, and his hands were all red and raw and they had patches of skin gone," Opal Majors volunteered from underneath the hair dryer.

"Dale said the exact same thing," Dolores Hinshaw said. "He thinks he has leprosy."

Opal unconsciously wiped her hand on her dress.

"I guess he's been getting treatments every Wednesday," Karen noted.

"For all the good it's doing, he might as well stay home and spend his last days with his family," Opal said.

Spurred on by this human tragedy, they recalled other grisly deaths they had encountered over the course of their lives and left the Kut 'n' Kurl immensely cheered by their own good health, except for Opal Majors, who rushed home and phoned Dr. Neely to see whether or not leprosy was contagious.

By the time Sam reached home, the pain had abated somewhat, though he still couldn't walk upright. He staggered in the kitchen door and bellowed for his wife. He lurched into the living room and collapsed on the couch just as she entered the room.

She sat on the floor beside him, stroking his stubbled head, barely able to speak.

"It's my back. I was helping Johnny Mackey carry chairs and I got twisted around and my back gave out."

It would be like this, she knew that now. Just the other day, in the produce aisle at the Kroger, Karen Grant had, with an uncanny prescience, described his last days. "Barbara, he'll get brittle on you and start snapping bones. That's how it always ends. By the time they die, they're like a lump of Jell-O."

"Do you want me to call Dr. Neely and get him over here?" she asked.

"Naw, it'll work its way out. It always has before."

He rolled off the couch and made his way across the room to the doorway, raising himself up along the door-jamb, hand over hand, until he could grasp the top of the door frame. He raised his legs and dangled in the doorway, twisting this way and that until his backbone realigned itself with a satisfying *pop!*

"Whew! Much better."

But Barbara was not consoled and knew that Sam's relief was temporary at best, a brief respite from the pain that would eventually reduce him to a vestige of his former self.

He swung his arms back and forth, then stretched. "Glad to be done with that," he said.

"Why don't you stay home for the rest of the day?" Barbara pleaded.

"Wish I could, honey, but I've got to get some things done."

Christmas was a scant five days away, and he and Frank were only half finished with the scrapbook.

"Will you be home for supper?"

"Probably not. I'll be going to my Wednesday night men's group. I'll just grab something on the way. Mind if I take the car?"

"Of course not."

He kissed her good-bye. She clung to him, her hold on him a lingering one. He hugged her back.

"I love you. You know that, don't you?" she asked him.

"I love you too, honey."

"I'll be thinking of you tonight. I'll wait up for you."

Women sure are funny, Sam thought, driving back to the meetinghouse. A month ago she was so mad she'd hardly speak to him, and now she was fawning all over him. Oh well, might as well enjoy it.

Frank was waiting for him at the office.

They spent the next five hours, until nine o'clock, affixing pictures onto the scrapbook sheets, arranging the letters, and applying a variety of stickers and borders.

"I think I'm getting the hang of this," Sam said.

"It sure is nice. Wish I could be there to see her face when she gets it," Frank said wistfully.

"No reason you can't be," Sam said.

"You mean it?"

"Sure, come on by. I'll wait until you're there before I give it to her."

Sam paused and thought for a moment, then grinned. "Hey, I got an idea. The boys get us up pretty early and we exchange gifts around seven, then have a nice breakfast around nine. Why don't I run over to Kivett's and get her some pot holders and wrap them up and give them to her first thing in the morning and she'll think that's her present. Then you come for breakfast and I'll give her the scrapbook after we've eaten."

"You sure I wouldn't be in the way?"

"Not at all," Sam assured him. "It'll be fun. Besides, if it weren't for you, I wouldn't even have had a scrapbook to give her."

"Well, I don't know about that. You'd have figured it out eventually," Frank said, now in an expansive mood.

Sam glanced at his watch. "Say, I better get going. Barbara's waiting up for me."

"Think she has any idea?"

Sam pondered Frank's question. "I haven't told anybody. Have you?"

"Not a soul," Frank promised, raising his right hand.

"This is the best gift I've ever given her," Sam said. "I only wish I had thought of it sooner. I hope she likes it."

It was all Frank could do not to break down. Here Sam was, dying by the inches, facing his last Christmas, and uppermost in his mind was his wife's happiness. He stood and embraced Sam, patting him on the back. "She's gonna love it, buddy. Don't you worry about that. She'll treasure it forever." His eyes filled with tears, and he wiped them away hastily before Sam could notice.

On his way home, Sam stopped by Kivett's Five and Dime just as Ned Kivett was locking the front door.

"What can I do for you, Sam?"

"Oh, just wanted to pick up a little something for Barbara. But I can see you're closing up shop. I'll stop by tomorrow."

Sam's back was starting to ache again. A slight spike of pain caused him to wince. Ned's heart sank. He'd known Sam since he was a child, and now this. At this rate, Sam probably won't even be around tomorrow, Ned thought. He unlocked the door. "Sam, I'm never closed for you. You take all the time you need."

I love Christmas, Sam thought happily. Everybody's so nice to each other.

"Thank you, Ned. I'll only be a minute." Sam walked back to the notions department, where the pot holders and dish towels were kept. On the shelf above the pot holders were the pelican sponge holders, one of which he'd purchased the year before. Next to them were a flock of pink porcelain flamingos. Sam picked one up and studied it.

"What's this?"

"Oh, that's real nice. It's a ring holder. A lot of the ladies take their rings off when they're washing dishes. See, they can just slide their rings right over the flamingo's head and down its neck. The pelican and the flamingo are a set."

"I got her the pelican last year."

"The flamingo would make a nice addition," Ned suggested. "The white and the pink look real good together."

"I'll get it," Sam said.

"Got a real nice flamingo pot holder and dish towel set to go with it," Ned said.

"Why not," Sam said. "It's Christmas only once a year."

"Want me to have Racine gift-wrap that for you? No charge. She can deliver it to the meetinghouse. Save you a little trouble."

"Sure, Ned. Thanks a bunch. I appreciate it."

Ned reached out and grasped Sam's hand. "I think you made a nice choice, Sam. Every time Barbara washes the dishes, she'll think of you." Ned struggled to keep his composure.

Sam tried to pay for the items, but Ned wouldn't let him. "You just take care of yourself. That's the only pay I need."

He walked Sam to the door, patting his back, then hugged him, squeezing him extra hard until he remembered Sam's feeble condition and loosened his grip.

When Sam arrived home, the boys were in bed and Barbara was asleep on the couch. There was a note on the kitchen table. *Sam, I made you a pie. It's in the refrigerator. Help yourself.* It was coconut cream, Sam's favorite, and he ate two pieces, thoroughly pleased with the affectionate turn in Barbara's disposition. Coconut cream pie! He washed his plate and fork and then nudged Barbara awake. They went upstairs, brushed their teeth, and fell into bed. Sam fell asleep promptly.

Barbara lay beside him, watching him, already starting to feel the ache of loneliness when he'd be gone. She rubbed her hand tenderly over his nubby head. Maybe it was her imagination, but he appeared to be losing weight. I'll make him another pie tomorrow, she vowed.

The next morning, he rose early, fed the boys their breakfast, and walked them to school, stopping by his parents' house afterward for a cup of coffee. They were seated at the kitchen table, discussing their Christmas plans and making small talk.

"Say, been meaning to ask you something," Sam's father said. "I was down at the hardware store last week, and Uly Grant starts talking about you and all of a sudden he starts tearing up. Did you and him have a falling-out or something?"

"No, not that I know of."

Of course, Sam's parents knew nothing of his looming departure, since people were reluctant to bring up this painful matter in their presence.

"It's the holidays, I think," Sam's mom said. "Everyone seems more emotional. Yesterday at the Kroger, Miriam Hodge hugged me right in front of the bacon."

"Yeah, and Asa Peacock told me this past Saturday if I needed any help with anything, to let him know," Sam's father said. "Then he starts rubbin' me on the back. Right there in the Co-op, in front of all the guys."

"It's the holidays," Sam agreed. "Yesterday, Ned Kivett wouldn't let me pay for the Christmas presents I got for Barbara."

"What'd you get her?" Sam's mother asked.

"A flamingo ring holder, with a matching dish towel and pot holder."

His father whistled. "Pretty nice."

"Got her something else too," Sam said. "Can you keep a secret?"

"Sure," they said in unison, then leaned forward. Sam knew for a fact they couldn't keep a secret better than anyone else in town.

"So can I," he said, with a laugh.

His father frowned. "That's a terrible way to treat your parents."

"Oh, you'll find out soon enough. Why don't you come over to the house for breakfast on Christmas morning? Around nine or so."

"Anything to keep from cooking," his mother said. "We'll be there."

Sam drank the last bit of his coffee, then set the cup in the sink. "Well, better go earn my keep."

It was a pleasant morning, and in Sam Gardner's little corner of the world, life was nearly perfect. The sun was up and shining, the television station was predicting six inches of snow on Christmas Eve, and after seventeen Christmases together, Sam was finally giving Barbara something she might actually like.

Preoccupied with thoughts of the Yuletide, he didn't notice the sidewalk curb, and his foot rolled over the edge. He felt a fantastic bolt of pain flare in his foot, and he toppled to the pavement, coming to rest against the wheels of Kathy's car. Kathy just the day before at the Kut 'n' Kurl had been lamenting Sam's deterioration.

She helped him to his feet and offered, over his strenuous objections, to drive him to the hospital.

"I'll be all right. Just a little banged up, that's all. I'll be fine."

It was all she could do not to cry. Twenty years in the hair-cutting business had acquainted her with human suffering, but this was too much. "Let me at least take you home."

"No need. Besides, I've got to get my work done. If you could drop me off at the office, that'll be fine."

Against her better judgment, she delivered him to the meetinghouse, helped him inside, and turned him over to Frank, then hurried to the Kut 'n' Kurl to inform her customers of Sam's worsening condition. "I tell you, seeing him laying on the street, his head up against my car tire, it was all I could do not to break down right then and there."

Even Bea Majors, who'd never really cared for Sam and was in that morning to have her eyebrows plucked for Christmas, felt a rare pang of sympathy. "I just don't understand why the Lord doesn't go ahead and take him," she said, shaking her head and pondering anew the vagaries of divine mercy.

SEVEN
The Nicest Gift Ever

The morning of Christmas Eve found Sam Gardner asleep in his living room recliner unable to negotiate the stairs to his bedroom. After two days of seeing Sam hobble around, Barbara had insisted he visit Dr. Neely, who'd referred him to Dr. Osborn, the town veterinarian and owner of the only X-ray machine in town.

"Congratulations, Mr. Gardner," Dr. Osborn told him, while studying the X-ray film. "There are twenty-six bones in the human foot, and you've broken three of them. But it could be worse."

"What could be worse than this?" Sam asked glumly.

"Just last week I had a horse with a similar break, and we had to put him down."

"Guess there's a bright side to everything," Sam said.

He shipped Sam back over to Dr. Neely's office, where his foot was put in a cast.

"I want you off your feet until after Christmas," Dr. Neely ordered. "Avoid stairs if at all possible. Don't want you falling and breaking your neck. I want you back here the first week of February and we'll take another look at it. If we can, we'll remove the cast then. If not, you'll need to wear it a few more weeks."

It was Sam's fourth day in the recliner, and he was crazy with boredom.

"The worst thing is, I won't get to see the progressive Nativity scene," he grumbled on Christmas Eve morning.

"I thought you said it was stupid and you wished Dale wouldn't do it," Barbara pointed out.

"I still like seeing everyone," Sam said. "And I'll miss the hot chocolate and cookies."

He spent the day watching television, which didn't improve his mood. Barbara made him his favorite lunch, tomato soup and grilled cheese, then gave him a back rub until he fell asleep with a slight, wiffling snore.

When he woke at six o'clock, a light snow was beginning to fall. It was dark outside and he could see the snowflakes fall against the light of the streetlamp in front of their home.

His suffering cast a pall over their home; his sons were avoiding him as if he were week-old roadkill, so foul was his mood.

At six thirty, their doorbell rang. "Go away," Sam yelled from his chair.

There was a loud clatter of activity in the front hallway. Sam could hear Frank the secretary laughing and his sons pleading for a ride.

"What's going on in there?" Sam yelled.

"Come on, Sam. We're going to see the progressive Nativity scene," Frank said, pushing a wheelchair into the living room. "Look what Johnny Mackey loaned me."

Barbara was standing in the doorway, verging on tears, contemplating what she suspicioned would be her husband's last Christmas.

Frank eased Sam from his recliner and steadied him as he hopped to the wheelchair. Barbara arranged his jacket around him, pulled a stocking cap over his pale head, then draped a blanket over his legs to protect the cast from the snow.

"Now all I need is to be hooked up to an IV so I'll look completely like an invalid," he muttered under his breath.

The boys ran to the front closet to retrieve their coats. Frank led the way, pushing the wheelchair, with one son on Sam's lap and the other holding the door open. They rolled out onto the front porch, bumped down the three steps and wheeled their way up the sidewalk, toward Uly Grant's house, the first stop of the progressive Nativity scene.

"This sure is nice of you, Frank," Sam said, slightly cheered by the change of scenery.

"Remember that when it comes time for my annual review," Frank said.

There was a crowd of Harmonians gathered on the sidewalk in front of Uly Grant's home, peering at the Baby Jesus, who was wrapped in swaddling clothes and lying in the manger.

The crowd parted as Sam approached, and Frank wheeled him to the front. People clucked their tongues sympathetically, then turned away, unable to bear the sight of their beloved pastor in what appeared to be his last days.

"What's that sign say?" Frank asked, squinting, pointing at a sign hanging directly over the Blessed Infant.

Sam peered at the sign. *Mattress Compliments of Bud's Mattress City! Mattresses Fit for a King! And the King of Kings!*

Sam groaned.

"Pretty sweet deal," Dale Hinshaw exclaimed, coming up behind him. "Got a free mattress, plus Bud donated all the hot chocolate, in exchange for putting up his sign."

Dale leaned closer to Sam. "What's Dr. Neely saying?"

"First week of February at the earliest. Maybe a few weeks past that, but no later."

Dale gasped. Though he'd never been an ardent supporter of Sam's, he certainly didn't wish him ill. He hurried home to inform his wife, pausing along the way to confirm everyone's deepest fear, that Sam was not long for this world. "Middle of February, tops," he announced to clusters of people, drawing his finger across his throat.

After viewing the Christ child, Frank and the Gardners made their way to Bea Majors's driveway to see Mary and Joseph, from there to Mabel Morrison's home to observe the wise men, then on to Dale's to view the shepherds abiding with their flocks.

Everywhere they went, they were greeted with kindly gestures and muffled sobs. They pushed on toward the meetinghouse, leaving a crowd of weeping citizens in their wake.

The hot chocolate was superb. Fern Hampton poured a mug for Sam, while Miriam Hodge presented him with a plate of chocolate chip cookies, warm from the oven. A strand of melted chocolate draped over his lower lip. He licked at it contentedly.

Sitting in the church basement, surrounded by his family and friends, Sam was as happy as he had been in months, which made everyone else all the more miserable as they marveled at his bravery in the face of certain death.

They stayed another hour, then Frank wheeled him home through the falling snow.

"What a perfect Christmas Eve," Sam announced as they drew close to home. "Can't thank you enough, Frank."

Frank patted him on the shoulder. "Don't mention it, little buddy. I'm glad I could do it."

He pushed Sam inside and deposited him in his recliner. "Johnny Mackey said you can use the wheelchair for as long as you need it."

"Tell him I appreciate it," Sam said. "I shouldn't need it very long."

Frank bit his hand to keep from crying.

Sam arranged himself in the recliner for a night's sleep. Barbara fussed over him, adjusting his blankets and plumping his pillow, then retired to their bed upstairs. She didn't sleep for worrying about Sam and finally rolled out of bed at six to begin cooking. By seven the boys were up and ripping through their presents, and by seven fifteen they were sprawled on the living-room floor in a gift-induced haze.

Sam watched on from his recliner, happy and amused by his sons. Barbara presented him with a genuine mother-of-pearl pocketknife. "I got it from the hardware store. Uly had to special order it." Sam loved pocketknives and was exceedingly pleased.

He reached underneath his blankets, pulled out a gift-wrapped package, and presented it to her. She smiled. "You did a wonderful job wrapping it."

"Thank you," he said, smiling modestly, forgetting to mention Racine Kivett had wrapped it.

She pulled the pink porcelain flamingo from its box and studied it curiously.

"It's a ring holder. The rings go over its head and down its neck," he explained. "It goes with the pelican sponge holder I gave you last year."

"So it does. And look, a matching pot holder and dish towel," she said, pulling them from the box.

Sam beamed from his recliner.

"Thank you, honey." She stood and leaned over him, kissing the top of his bristly head.

Frank and Sam's parents arrived a little before nine and even though Sam had forgotten to tell Barbara he'd invited them, she took it in good stride, it being Sam's last Christmas and all.

By ten thirty they had finished eating and had washed the dishes, threw away the wrapping paper, and were stretched out in the living room, as bloated as ticks.

Sam could hardly stand it. Four months of hard work and sacrifice—glue in his hair, his hands scrubbed red and raw, the utter humiliation visited upon him by Mrs. Hilda Gruber, the scorn heaped on by his fellow scrapbookers. But it had all been worth it. And now his moment in the sun had arrived, his fifteen minutes of gift-giving fame.

"Say, Levi," he said to his older son, "I think I forgot to give your mommy one of her presents. Is there something under the couch?"

Levi lifted the skirt of upholstery at the bottom of the couch and fished a substantial box out from underneath it.

"Well, would you look at that," Sam said. "I nearly forgot it."

Frank looked on, on the verge of rupturing he was so excited.

"This is for me?" Barbara said, holding it in her lap and raising it up and down to judge the weight of it.

"Yours and no one else's," Sam said proudly.

She untied the ribbon and peeled off the tape. Sam was a big believer in tape, and it took her a while. She pulled back the wrapping and studied the scrapbook, a bit puzzled. She opened the first page and gasped, then turned the page. She began to cry. "Oh, Sam. This is wonderful. Just beautiful. Who did this for you?"

"What do you mean who did it? I did it," Sam said, with no small amount of pride.

"I helped some too," Frank said, unable to contain himself.

She continued turning the pages. "Oh, here are the boys. And here I am, just a little kid. Where'd you get that picture?"

"Your mom sent some up."

"Oh, Sam. This is the best Christmas present I've ever gotten. This was so thoughtful."

"He's a chip off the old block, that's for sure," Sam's dad said.

"Yep, it took lots of Wednesday nights, but I finally got it done," Sam said.

It took a moment for Sam's comment to register with Barbara. She looked up from her scrapbook. "What did you say?"

"I said it took a lot of Wednesday nights, but I finally got it done," Sam repeated.

"You weren't going to a men's group?"

"No, sorry, honey. Didn't like lying to you, but I had to keep it secret. I was taking a scrapbooking class in Cartersburg." He paused, weighing whether he should reveal the sordid details, then decided to make a clean sweep of things. "But I had a small accident with some glue, got it stuck in my hair. That's why I had to get my hair cut. And Hilda Gruber, she was the teacher, she threw me out, so Frank helped me finish."

"I learned how to scrapbook from my daughter and granddaughters," Frank volunteered. "They're taking a class in it."

"You weren't in a men's group?" Barbara asked again.

"Nope."

"Do you have cancer?" she asked.

"Not that I'm aware of," Sam answered, genuinely puzzled by her questions.

"Are you sick at all?"

"My foot hurts a bit, but I'll be okay."

"You feel perfectly fine?" she asked.

"If I was any better, I'd be twins," Sam said, smiling.

"Sam Gardner, I could throttle you." She spoke each word clearly and distinctly, in a way eerily reminiscent of Mrs. Hilda Gruber. Then she began to cry. "Sam, I thought you were dying. I thought you were going to the hospital for treatments on Wednesday nights."

Sam's father began to cackle. His wife cuffed him upside the head. "Shame on you. Barbara's been worried sick. That's not funny."

"You're absolutely right," Sam's father said, composing himself. "Sam, you oughta be ashamed of yourself. Worrying your wife like that."

Frank stared at Sam, dumbfounded. "You mean I've been waiting on you hand and foot, fetching you hamburgers and coffee and aspirin, and here you are, healthy as a horse?"

"Don't think I didn't appreciate it," Sam said. "It was awfully kind of you."

"I should have stayed on strike," Frank said glumly.

To his dismay, Sam's declaration of health was received like a bucket of cold water in the face. The rest of the day passed slowly, with Sam in his recliner and Barbara sticking her head in the doorway every now and again to glare at him.

"Mommy's really mad at you," their son Addison reported midway through the day.

"Certain people around here wouldn't be happy unless I were dying," Sam yelled in Barbara's general direction.

She chose not to dignify his comment with a response.

She went to bed at nine o'clock without telling him goodnight. A half hour later, he dragged himself up the stairs to their bedroom, letting his cast bump loudly against each step in hopes of waking her up. He dropped into bed beside her and lay still, except for an occasional exaggerated sigh.

He was determined not to be the first one to speak. Several minutes passed before he realized she was still asleep. He nudged her awake, then pretended to be sleeping.

"Sam, did you wake me up?"

"What?" He blinked his eyes and feigned confusion. "Were you talking to me?"

After seventeen years of marriage, she knew all his tricks. She punched him on the arm.

They lay on their backs, staring at the ceiling. Then she

turned toward him, settling into the crook of his arm. She thumped him lightly on the chest. "You knucklehead. I thought you were dying."

"Sorry to disappoint you. Next time you think I'm dying, I'll try to accommodate you."

She flipped on the light beside her bed, reclined against the headboard, retrieved her scrapbook from the nightstand, and began thumbing through it with Sam.

"I can't believe you did this," she said.

"It was pure genius, if I do say so myself," Sam said, fighting to be modest, but losing the battle.

He pulled her closer as she turned another page.

"Why did you put this picture in here?"

"Hey, not everybody gets crowned the Lawrence County Tenderloin Queen. I think you looked cute."

"You don't think I looked fat?" she asked.

"Not at all."

"I wished I still looked like that," Barbara said, studying the picture.

"Not me," Sam said. "You were cute then. You're beautiful now."

"Oh, Sam."

"So who else thinks I'm dying?" Sam asked. "Did you tell anyone?"

"Just Frank. He promised to keep it a secret."

Sam sighed.

She pulled him to her and kissed him flush on the lips, which Sam assumed, correctly in this instance, indicated an appetite for more serious snuggling, which he endeavored, crippled as he was, to satisfy.

"So you liked your present?" he asked afterward.

"Yes, the flamingo was lovely."

"I mean the scrapbook."

"It's the best gift I've ever gotten." But even as she said it, she knew it wasn't true. The best gift was having him beside her.

"I knew you'd like it," he said, smiling in the dark.

He fell asleep that way, in the trough of their double bed, the quilts stacked deep upon them, the wind rattling like death through the skeletal trees. Barbara laid her head against Sam's chest, consoled by the sturdy *thump-ka-thump* of his heart.

She was too preoccupied to sleep. She pulled a quilt off their bed and, wrapping it around herself, sat in the rocker beside the window. Outside the snow began to fall again, the wind picked up, painting swirls of snow on the street and reshaping them a few seconds later with another gust, which Barbara thought somehow symbolized life. The winds of Providence blow where they will, and it's wise to enjoy the loveliness while one can.

SERVING HARMONY, INDIANA

Harmony Herald

Tuesday, January 13, 2004

Town Gets New Hydrant

Bobservation Post by Bob Miles

Your Two Cents Worth

Register for your free subscription to the Harmony e-newspaper

Harmony Herald

Go to www.harmonyherald.com

ALSO BY PHILIP GULLEY

Fiction

Home to Harmony

Just Shy of Harmony

Signs and Wonders: A Harmony Novel

Life Goes On: A Harmony Novel

A Change of Heart

Nonfiction

Hometown Tales

Front Porch Tales

For Everything a Season

If Grace Is True *(with James Mulholland)*

If God Is Love *(with James Mulholland)*

Want to receive notice of events and new books by Philip Gulley? Log on to Philip Gulley's Web site at www.philipgulleybooks.com